Dog

Dog wants to play.

2

# Frogs hop. Can Dog hop too?

Hop

Hop

Hop

FLOP

# Frogs leap. Can Dog leap too?

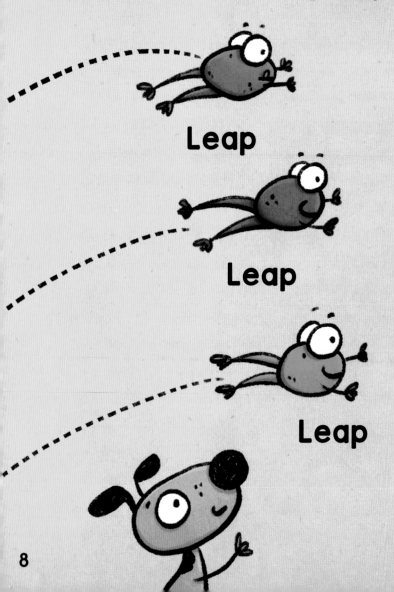

Leap

Leap

Leap

# Frogs jump. Can Dog jump too?

Jump

Jump

Jump

Jump

13

Dog will play another day.

19

21

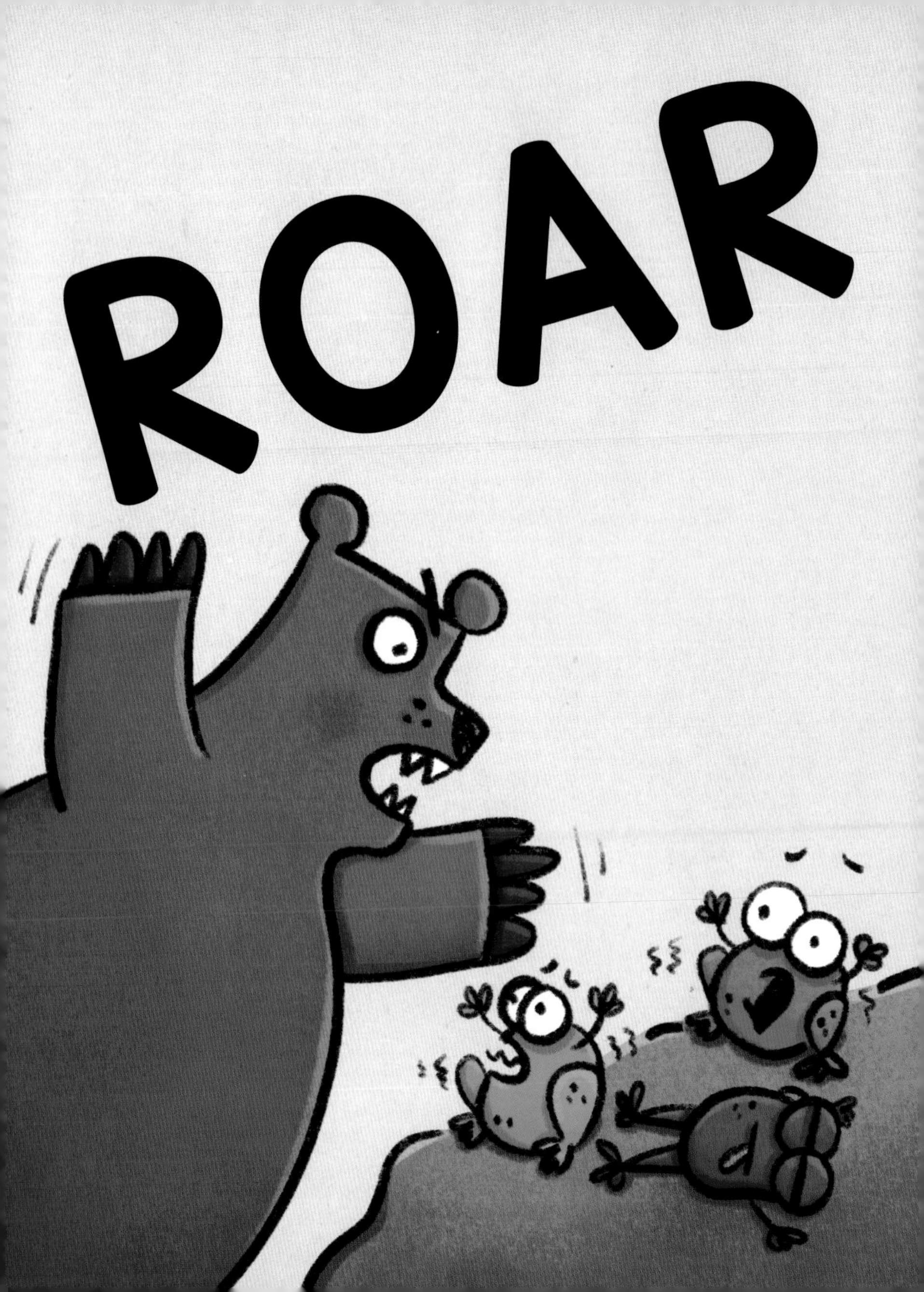
ROAR

# Dog wants to help.
# How can Dog help?

Jump

Jump

Jump

Frogs want to play.

# Frogs hop. Can Dog hop too?

Hop

Hop

Hop

DROP

38

# Frogs leap. Can Dog leap too?

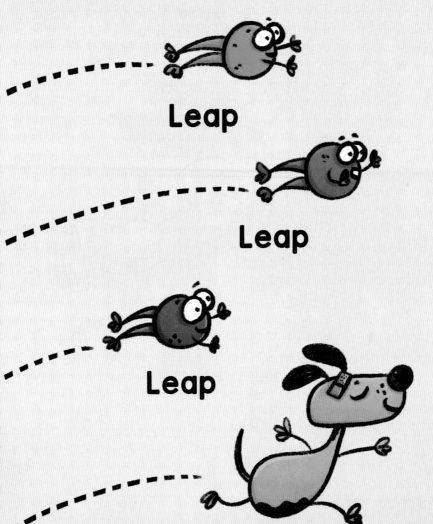

Leap

Leap

Leap

Heap

# Sleep

Bzzzzz ...

Frog wants to eat.

42

43

Dog will play another day.

# About the Author

**Janee Trasler** loves to make kids laugh. Whether she is writing books, drawing pictures, singing songs, or performing with her puppets, she is going for the giggle. Janee lives in Texas with her hubby, her doggies, and one very squeaky guinea pig.

# YOU CAN DRAW FROG!

**1** Draw a sideways figure of eight.

**2** Add a dot in the middle of each circle. Draw a "u" for the mouth.

**3** Connect the eyes with a big circle for the body.

**4** Add an oval on each side for the legs. Draw two little feet.

**5** Draw the arms and hands. Be sure to add some speckles!

**6** Colour in your drawing!

# WHAT'S YOUR STORY?

Dog plays with the frogs.
Imagine **you** are playing with them.
What games would you play together?
Write and draw your story!